MW01231923

AN
OVERTURE
OF LIGHT

AN
OVERTURE
OF LIGHT

CALVIN MILLER

WORD PUBLISHING
Dallas · London · Vancouver · Melbourne

AN OVERTURE OF LIGHT

Library of Congress Cataloging-in-Publication Data

Miller, Calvin
    An overture of light / by Calvin Miller
      p. cm.
    Final vol. in Symphony trilogy: sequel to: A symphony in sand and A requiem for love.
    ISBN 0-8499-0689-X
    I. Title.
PS3563.I37609 1991
811'.54—dc20
                                  91-15149
                                    CIP

Printed in the United States of America

1 2 3 4 9 AGF 9 8 7 6 5 4 3 2 1

In him was life,
and that life was the light of men.
The light shines in the darkness,
but the darkness has not understood it.
                        John 1:4, 5 NIV

Their swords were wet
With tears not blood.
Michael swung at Lucifer
And Lucifer stabbed back.
But here and there they laid aside their
    swords,
Embraced and wept for their lost
    brotherhood,
Then picked their grieving weapons up
To fight again their war of tears.
It was a Lover's Armageddon.

I

My dearest Krystar,
Here at the end of time
I must write to you of its beginning
So you may bring to memory
How much your lust for power
Has cost our Father.
I can no longer fly to you on wings of hope.
The camps of dark and light
Are flung far separate and wide.
The battle soon is over.
Your War is all but lost!
Dear God, our Father, grieves your loss!
Are you pleased
That you've divided all immortal being
Into separate quarreling camps?
Can you see now
That Hell is any separation
That thrusts division into love?
Love moves with force
And yet is always delicate:
A porcelain exquisite bond
That cannot live
Unless all those who keep it
Honor what is precious
But easily destroyed.
Krystar, He gave this fragile love to us
Yet you, with rough despising
Threw it down and gloated on the shattering.
Thus, weeping came to our fair realm
Where God's rich laughter once held sway.

Why?

Do you have no regrets?
Does your faithless conscience ever burn
With any remorse I'd understand?
You made Heaven a high abyss!

It must be laid to your account!
You brought the walls and gates.
And so our Father's Hell was born!
He never wanted walls or gates.
He wanted only that His universe
Remain one open endless realm forever!

Krystar, He weeps—our Father weeps—
Each time He sees these gates.
One does get used to them in time
And I no longer ache on merely seeing them.
But if I think too long upon their true atrocity,
My mind bends double
And my heart breaks for
The great divorce you made—
Dividing good and evil, love and hate.

The gates, the gates! Eternal, never ending!
Where those immortal hinges swing dividing . . .
        separating,
Setting love inside, and hate without—
A great gulf there forever fixed between the two.
His once and glorious universe
Is now a changeling, quarreling, mutiverse
Because of your capricious greed.

Where are you these days, brother?
Still planning wars you cannot win?
Still building gates and separating wills?
Throwing walls between all lovers?
And what of those who left with you?
We call "them" aliens here.
"Them" was a short, yet heavy word
For all of us to learn—
Like gates, "them" was a word of strange division.
"Us" for all of those inside the gates,
"Them" for all of you who've gone,
Leaving nothing but the lonely wind blowing
Through the crystal habitations you despised.

Krystar, you wounded all the universe
With such division. Why? Forever, why?
It is a pointless question.
It does so little good to ask you "Why?"
And yet I must. Was Heaven not enough?
Was His Fatherhood so small a gift
That you'd prefer the empty orphanage of Hell
To live forever with no hope?
Why, when He gave you wonder
Did you wish He'd given power?
Sometimes I see you yet
On that foolish day of ego
When you begged Him for a throne.
It was a tantrum
Born from cosmic impudence!
Your starving lust
Was always hungry, never full,
Nor did it understand.
To have a throne but feeds the appetite
To have a better throne . . . a bigger throne . . .
To eliminate all other thrones!

He knew where your fierce need would lead.
That's why He begged you to be content.
He knew your thirst would
Deepen with your drinking.
That's why we all need Fathers—
To withhold the serpents
From our cradles
Even when we beg to have them.
Even now admit this truth!
Call Him gracious! Call Him kind!
For He withheld from you
Only what He knew
Would destroy you completely.
You should have asked a footstool
Where you could have sat to learn
What Godhood is and how servanthood

Is the only footstool which in time
Becomes a throne.

You do have a kind of throne, I suppose!
You rule in such little ways as may bring a devil joy.
And yet I wish that you were home
And things were as they used to be
When love knew no antithesis.

I am writing not to beg you to return.
Rather, I am calling to your mind
The glorious yesterdays that now divide us.
Not only Heaven was stabbed,
By your unyielding drives,
But Terra also sweltered under iron greed.
Was it necessary for you to plunge
The sword of death into Earth's blue ball
And bring it death and dying?

I trust you've not forgotten how you felt
When first you left our realm?
Remember how our Father grieved
To see His Terra cut and stabbed and scarred
By wounds that grew gigantic as the night.

I would remind you
As you read this last account
That soon your reign of death will end.
You have one final moment of brief glory—
And then the power you used to terrorize the worlds
Will all be stripped away.
The gates which we despise
Will once again be gone
And earth and Heaven will flow
Together like long-damned rivers of pure joy.

I ask you to remember
All you sacrificed upon the altar

Of your ego.
Remember this when judgment comes
Lest you are prone to cry
That He who made you is unfair.

Read on, Krystar, and tremble,
And make these memoirs glistening rebukes.
Start long before the start.
Begin before the great beginning.
Remember how He spoke of origins
And of those voices flying on the winds.

Before Adam, there were atoms,
And before atoms, nothing—Nihil.
Yet never was there truly nothing
For always in the empty dark
There lived a glorious promise—
A trace of salt
Upon the eager tongue of vacuum
That waited in a sea of nothingness
To taste what soon must come.

II

We are agreed," the Father said.

"We are indeed," the Spirit answered back.

"As we are one,
We'll fly as three," the Son replied.
And through the ethers of stark nothingness
The winds screamed in joyous darkness
Speaking to the universe unformed.

"Be!" cried the Father to the sterile womb of night.
And nothingness upon command stood ready
For the three to fly and offer their demands.

"I'll craft it," said the Father.
"I'll save it," said the Son.
"I'll fill it," said the Spirit.

Then to the unmade chaos the trio called:
"I can create and shall," the Father said.
"I can redeem and shall," the Son agreed.
"I can bind all as one . . . and shall," the Spirit uttered.

And on they flew,
One God in trilogy
With His own glorious inwardness.
"I shall have children and proclaim my Fatherhood."
The Father laughed in joy.

"I shall have brothers and clasp them as my family."
The Son laughed, too.

"I shall bring communion to this family,
Binding up the many parts of universal being,
Forbidding all division!"
The Spirit exulted.

They spoke of all they'd be
Once nothingness had yielded:
"I shall give up sole volition—
Sovereign and undisputed
To create the precious
Gift of human will," the Father said,
"That all who live may know
How glorious it is to be like God
And deep within the self to choose."

"I shall give up my own right
Of self-protection and wear
Such wounds as flesh may know,"
The Son replied.

"I shall lead all who will
To turn from mere mortality
To become a part of everything enduring,"
The Spirit called.

"I'll make," said the Father.
"I'll bleed," said the Son.
"I'll touch," said the Spirit.

"All shall be here," said the Father.
"All shall be safe," said the Son.
"All shall be one," said the Spirit.

"Here's to human being."
"Here's to human meaning."
"Here's to human hoping."

The Spirits merged and separated,
Throbbed, expanded, and then settled into one.
As one they waited, ordering the future.

"Then is our cosmic drama set,"
The Spirit One in Three declared.
"The actors are in place.

The star is set in space.
This empty void is a disgrace.
In love . . . we shall this void displace."

They flew as one, as three, as one.
And yet as breezes may be separate
They blew all individually
And yet remained a single wind.
Three voices crying out as one,
"I'll order the worlds to be."
"I'll call the worlds to Me."
"I'm light, that worlds may see."

"I'll sigh, 'It is begun!'"
"I'll say, 'It has been done!'"
"I'll bind all things as one."

And in a cosmic final shout they cried,
"Let emptiness and nothingness give way.
Night flies before the driving light of day."

Loneliness is a granite anvil
On which the chains
Of all relationships are forged.

III

And so it was before we came.
Thus did the flying Spirit's
Breathe their dreams o'er emptiness.
I must recount for you, Krystar,
The way it all began.
Oh, brother, lay aside your sword
And marvel at this dream you have unraveled.

"In the beginning nothing lived
Except the Father-Spirit.
Living . . . as He ever lived . . .
Aching in His need to touch
A particle of anything beyond Himself.
Some atom gathered deep within His being.
His Spirit-fingers, plasma filtering,
Felt through the nothingness, embracing cold.
Our Father was aroused with lust for company.
God groaned and reaching after life,
He stretched in powerful yearnings.
"I am Sovereignty without a kingdom . . .
Fatherhood in search of children.
I starve for uncreated otherness,
I soar above the vacuum of my making
Crying hungrily, 'I've come—
Come anything to meet me!
Emptiness be gone!'"

His lusty words copulated with
The cancer-cold of emptiness,
Like lavish lava from a generous inferno,
Till His conceiving love
Had planted life within the mocking womb of vacancy.

"Be born, sweet universe!
I will not live alone!"
The Father-Spirit cried.
"No heavens and no earth!

No place to meet Myself, come substance!
Give Me some pedestal
Where form may stand on emptiness—
A dais where My fertile and gigantic dreams
May find a place to hatch."

A bold and dazzling shelf of glass was born.
It was a wondrous frozen plane
Of warm transparency—
A see-through place for love to seek itself.
His threesome oneness had at last
A place to rest.
And resting on that crystal ledge
He cried again His one grand glittering command,
"Be!"

An embryo without umbilical
Tumbled through the void
And hurtled in an arc of light,
As unaborted being split in two.
"I am a Father unto nothingness—
Yet Fathers cannot be if sons are not.
Come life!"

The empty stratosphere drew back
And thus allowed two other wombless embryos
To pass the birth-canal of emptiness.

Oh, Krystar . . . can you not remember
Our ecstasy at being born all of a sudden?
We came apace upon the heels of nothingness,
Like children of old promises we came.
We were twin spirit-boys who cried.
We shivered, nude with newness,
For the stars were not yet made
And the emptiness He set to frame us
Was ice-crusted like a foolish planet
Which wanders much too far beyond its mother sun.

Our thin and needy infant wail
Grew at last to thunder that
Tore His cosmos with the glorious sound of life.
Crying sons, we were, new-born in space!
Our Father reached toward us
And laid His wondrous hand
Upon our piercing wails
And all the universe around was hushed
By love's first miracle of touch.
We thus began to grow
And ages fell like seconds
In voids that knew no clocks.
We lengthened, slept and passed to manhood
In the mist of time-warped mysteries.

There is a lie that circulated
On Terra in her former days.
Some said that life came
When nature birthed itself in
Fiery cold phenomena that acted on its own.
Ah, but we know the truth, don't we?
All life comes from Spirit
Whether they be dumb and thankless organisms
Or poets singing to the stars,
Dumbfounded by their steady courses.
Only where the Spirit lives
Is the soil deep enough for life to find a root.
And any life too proud to dip its roots in Spirit soil
Does not merely die, it never comes to be.

The Father-Spirit's joy swelled
Pervading black and cold with everlasting hope.
His crystal shelf of being
Melted into liquid silicate.
His hot tears scalded cosmic ice.
He doted on the frigid emptiness.

Then like a confident midwife
He reached to bring forth His child.
He thrust His dreams in fingers of hot fire
Into the darksome womb of His desire.

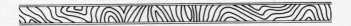

Cain never meant to kill his brother
And so was quite surprised
To see him lying pulseless on the sod.
He only meant to prove by crushing skulls
Who was the better friend of God.

IV

I remember now . . .
I raised myself upon one hand
And blinked into the swirling mist
That blew in spirit eddies
Around my new awareness.
I marveled that with no one there
To teach me, I knew I had a name
And knew what that name was.
"I am Ansond," I cried.
And reached my hand to touch your own.

You, brother, stirred the mist
Around our rising naked forms, "I am Krystar,
Called to life from nothingness!" you said.
Also untaught, you knew your name.

And we, the mist-made brothers, met,
Each a kind of image of the other.
Krystar, you stood as tall as morning
In that primeval light
A golden son . . . proud progeny to make
The great Almighty roar.

Your eyes were liquid bronze
That matched your golden skin.
My eyes were firelit-blue
As sky can sometimes blaze at sunrise.
Earthmaker cried to us swimming in the sterile dark,
"My sons, behold the birth of worlds!
This all-imprisoning night
Shall keep no eye in chains."

And thus, Krystar, He woke us
Unto life and glorious being.
God-made, we were, before the universe
Had ever come to be.

Half-roused in sluggish clouds
We stood at once above the mist
That now embraced our ankles,
We walked forward—
Reaching hands, extending fingers—
Until our fingers met.
All our emptiness knew instant glory!
For touching is the miracle
That dances open all the lonely gates of self.

"Ansond," you asked me then,
"Where is love? Do you remember?"

"It's in the light!" I cried,
"Love always comes in light!"

"Does anything exist that is not love?"

"Love has an opposite, as silence, sound,
But seek it not, lest what it is be found!"

"Surely you remember how we met?
We strode the shelf of space,
As thunder rattles glass
Or surf thrums tympani on ocean rocks.
We had come to be
And our hilarity at being overcame us.
We fell into a grand embrace,
Threw back our heads and laughed,
Spangling all the vacant night with joy.
At length we dropped our close embrace
And held each other distant,
And, staring eye to eye,
We turned our burning beam of vision upward.

"Where our searing sight rays met,
A star of laser gold became
A brilliant sun that settled

Ever downward with our gaze.
Slowly . . . slowly . . . slowly
Came the central sphere of light.
At its laser heart it held
A settling chair of gleaming glass,
That mortared itself upon a pedestal.
Our laughter was crushed to silence
By the whelming wonder.

"Do not stop laughing!"
The thunder of the Father-Spirit
Rumbled from the glass,
And roared like cosmic organ pipes
With twice our volume.
It was impossible not to join the joy!
And so,
Krystar, we joined the Crystal chair in laughter,
Filling all the void with sound—
Being, unashamed of being!

At length
The glass chair shouted,
"I am your Father-Spirit.
Praise is the only cure for emptiness.
Laughter is the footprint of My being,
Joy, My perfect portrait!"

His words in hurricanes of laughter
Made life swarm forth in raging gales of pride.
"See all that laughter makes," the storm replied.

Where the seen and unseen copulate
They sire a child named mystery.

V

Krystar, my brother,
Here at this war's beginning,
Remember, oh remember, and repent your pride.
We once were as gods, yet children
Of our forming Father—
Two of us, beloved and cherished
By our Lord and Maker.
We skipped as giants skip
From island unto island
Of some primeval ocean.
We hopscotched galaxies
And laughed above their tiny
Bragging suns adored by micro-worlds in orbit.

Our innocence was glorious!
How glorious we never knew.
Still after we had
Laughed a thousand years
I heard you crying.
There is no sin in crying, it's just that
Crying says there's something wanting in our lives.
What missing item was it
That brought your sobbing?
What was it that was absent
From His great supply?
Pick any planet,
And all of it was yours.
Fly about whole fields of stars
And name them as your treasure.
What was it that you lacked?
I tried to comfort you.
I begged you to be content.

"Do you believe our Father
Could make some
World for me alone to rule?"

You asked.
Your question troubled me.

"Of course, as He makes any sun or world."

"I want a place to rule
As my own special realm.
Some home that I can craft myself
And breed my kind in my own way.
I'd like to make myself a son
As He made me."

"Why do you want to be a maker?"
I asked.

"Because in all this glittering possibility of life
There are but makers and things made.
Things made are what we are.
Like Him who is our source
I would be one who makes,
And not merely what is made."

"Come then," I said, "Let's fly to Him
And ask Him if there is not such a place."
It troubled me to think
That you felt incomplete.
When all His love
Like jewels around your feet
Was waiting to be claimed.
We flew back to the gleaming shelf of glass
And waited for your emptiness to pass.

Power is strength, power is wonder.
Power's a jagged bolt of light
Fiercely wrapped in summer thunder.
How odd we pray to wooden gods,
Whose very hearts are
Oft made hollow by egoistic termites,
That gnaw at sanctity.

VI

When we returned we found
Our Father-Spirit laughing.
God's laughter always heals
And so your tears were dried.
Suddenly I, too, could laugh again.

Great God!
How good it felt to laugh:
The burdens which we think
Can only crush us, do with laughter
Yield up their iron weight
And dress themselves in feathers.
Angels fly, not because they have wings,
But because they laugh.

Things were suddenly made right.
You, too, began to laugh
And I forgot the old captive fears,
For you had put aside your emptiness
Signaling you felt complete again
And needed nothing but His love.
For a moment all the world seemed healed.
My anxious ill and its disquiet slept!
Still inwardly I wondered
Why a loving Father would build into our bodies
The possibility of wanting
Things that we could never own.

Why?

Don't you see, Krystar,
He could have made us love Him
By forbidding any hint of our rebellion—
By making us robotic angels blessing Him
Because we had no choice?
It struck me even then, Krystar,

That love without the right to choose
Isn't love at all.
Until love may withhold itself,
It may not choose to give itself.
And when it lacks either freedom
Whatever else it may be called
It cannot wear the name of love!

But for the moment
Peace had come to Heaven.
Your greed slept awhile!
Our Father-Spirit went on laughing
Till ultimately He cried,
"Lions, eagles, lightning!"

At His word two tawny lions came to be
And rose from gray, creating mists.
They roared and stalked the royal throne,
Like predators of grace,
Till each beast settled
By the glistening chair.
As powerful, jungle denizens,
Without a jungle where their lordship
Might proclaim itself.
They bore no terror or malignity.
At last, their burning feral eyes
Turned to amber crystal
That died in glass.

Then eagles came on thrashing wings.
Shattering the air with screaming
They fluttered down in grandeur
Upon the crested arches
High above the gleaming chair.
Their sepia splendor
Faded into blue-gray bronze,
Then froze—open winged—in shining steel
Above the throne of light.

I remember, brother, standing dumb
Before this storm of power,
Ashamed to break the hush.
It was you who dared to cry aloud,
Brashly like a selfish child,
"Oh, give me this!
My every appetite cries out,
I need . . . I need . . . I need."

Heaven's laughter died!

An icy wind froze all your final words.
"Father, Father . . . give me . . . give me!
I want my own glass chair
And power to cry out, 'Lions, Eagles, Lightning!'
And order what I will to be."

At your unbridled lust
Our realm looked down ashamed
And stared with a forbidding silence.

You fell to sobbing once again.
"Father, I need this power!
I want to be like You!
How can You call that love
Which leaves Your children so unsatisfied?
Will You always be the only one
Who can be called a 'maker'?"

Our Father looked away.

"Father," you went on,
"I want to make!
I want to rule some sector of this universe.
Give me a throne in some remote infinity.
So I may be like You.
Is it too great a thing to ask,
To laugh and order things to be?

Don't say You love me and refuse to give
Those very gifts that make me want to live."
The Father-Spirit never answered
Your ego-driven argument.
I've learned since then He never talks
To those who meet Him Ego first.
Rather, Heaven wrapped itself in quiet.
The chair of glass encased itself in lead
As though God's infant hope had been born dead.

Satan earned his name
The day he grabbed God's new-made sun
And stuck it in his pocket.
"Let me be God—let there be dark!" he
　　cried.
A crippled demiurge he thus became—
A small club-footed mini-god who
　　stumbled with a cane—
A palsied thing. And so, demented with
　　no mind,
Dark spectacled, he ruled the light, quite
　　blind.

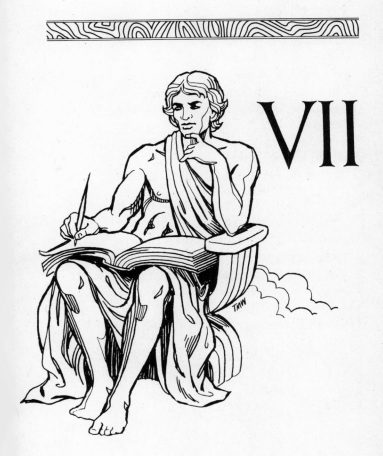

VII

And so, Krystar, we soon must finish
What was there begun.
I'm writing so that you may understand
A crucial truth that you have overlooked.
I will not see you taken
To your cold and final prison.
Misunderstanding . . . and you did misunderstand!
Your arrogance did not consider all the facts.
You fought our Blessed Father
In Heaven's civil war,
Unfurnished with the whole truth.
You can't undo your tangled knot of selfishness
That twisted age and empire in the cords.
The coiling labyrinthine course you ran
Snagged Heaven in the barbs
Then spiraled ever downward.

We could not speak of "down or up."
In those days of new being.
"Down and up" were really words like "us and them."
It took a while to learn to use them.
Down never spoke of being lower in position,
It only spoke of something less in being . . .
Down from His exalted throne . . .
Down to a lesser way of thinking and of loving.

Soon Heaven's hosts must fly at you
And finally set the universe at peace,
Tear down the gates,
Repair His broken Heaven.

You will not be killed!
That's the little way that
Humans end their countless Armageddons.
But you will be contained,
Sealed alive in being—nevermore to grow
And then reduced forever.

Each dawn you'll wake to find yourself
Smaller than you were the day before.
Little by little you will lose your soul
In a world where God forever grows in grandeur.

Diminished you will be,
Not by any act that makes you smaller,
But because your being will stay constant in its size
While Heaven grows around you.
In such an ever-growing universe,
You'll learn the truth
That there are two mere modes of being—
To die or grow—
And that to remain the same
While all else grows
Is but to die.

You will also learn
That dying, like living, is a process,
Begun the very moment we decide
That living requires too much of us.
For any life to grow it must
Adore the meat of discipline
And drink the broth of pain.
Dying's always easier than living,
Requiring nothing more than frequent rest
And easy gluttonies
That feed us everything we want.

Dying comes from blessing our addictions—
And watching others work.
Hiring porters for the luggage we find heavy
Or living off of our inheritance while leaving none
        behind.
It was not really a throne you desired.
It was a couch:
A place to luxuriate in power
While others served you.

You were chained by liberties
That grew into addictions.
So, Krystar, you will not die in war,
You'll perish slow 'neath piles of easy chains
You never disciplined yourself to break.

All lust is strong narcotic
Nominating different hungers
Which we suppose we need:
Wine, wantoness, food and leisure
All kill us one link at a time,
And in the coiling, spiraling steel
Inch by inch, they do require our lives.

Having lost the war of self-control
Your own apocalypse is now at hand!
Before the missiles fly
Look down and see the mountains of poor Terra.
These are those peaks where some few men and
       women
Learned nobility through faith in God.
Oh, that you had been as wise!
Here and there among the thousands
Were a few who knew that God's esteem
Was to be prized above all power.
They laid aside their need to rule
And named themselves His servants.
They turned their back upon the plains
And reached toward the heights.
They blessed the daily bread of Discipline.
They struggled upward, climbing
To unite themselves with God.
They rebuked their weary flesh
Till it no longer craved the level places.
They despised the easy life!
And struggled in the fiery love
They offered to our Father.
Their very throne was pilgrimage.

Their scepter was the single dream
Of pleasing their Creator.
They strove to gain His pleasure.
They made their tendons cry on screaming precipices
And pressed their cheeks tight against the granite
      cliffs.
They clung to tiny cracks
To raise their dying bodies
Toward the summits they defied.
When at last they stood atop the peak,
They had not merely climbed,
They had taught their sluggish egos
To postpone their deaths awhile.

Krystar, you turned your back upon the climb,
Despised the Discipline of struggle.
You chose the ease of living in the plains.
Oh, that you would have been more wise,
Rebuked your lust to have and reached to claim
Those heights He planned for you.

Behold the aerie vistas
Of His wondrous love
And weep for that plain chaff
You traded diamonds to obtain.
Oh, do remember what you chose to be
And what was lost to obscene irony!

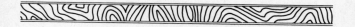

Cinderella may have ruled the ball
But she saved no one but herself.
Abused by selfish sisters
She learned no greater lessons
Than to become like them herself,
Wanting only what they wanted:
To dance and to be queen.

VIII

I recall for you again
The day the Hosts were born.
Our Father-Spirit's breath commanded, "Be!"
The ordered mist again brought forth—
And bountifully.
Bold beings rose from the fragile birthing clouds.
Angels—Titan creatures like ourselves—
Came to being in countless white battalions
A hundred, then ten thousand, .
Then glistening hordes beyond all numbering.

How many came? It matters not.
These were our brothers!
Though I could see you wanted them
Not as your brothers
But as subordinates and poor commodities
For uses you could make of them.
I saw them as our equals to be loved.
You saw them as mere fodder
For those causes you devised.

The mists then cleared and lifted
As though the vapors, having made
A million creatures
Had served enough
And now were free!
The Father laughed and called to us!
"Ansond, Krystar!
Here, My firstborn sons,
Are your companions,
Born as mystic nations all at once.
Be not alone." He called to us.
"Thrive and laugh as one.
The universe is great enough for all."

I thrilled exultingly as I beheld
The standing fields of shining souls.

I was stunned by your behavior!
What made you turn in sullen rage?
You must have known your anger
Would embarrass Heaven.

"Love!" you screamed!
"And yet no chair for me. Why Father-Spirit?
Must You insult us
With a field of children?
Are we not enough?
Must You make more and more
And diminish our importance
By adding millions of adorers?
Your greedy need for lovers
Keeps all of us in weariness.
Your crystal tricks but fondle Your preeminence
And steal all our dignity.
Almighty in Your power, almighty in Your ego!
You create fields of slaves
And then misname our fallen caste as lovers."

"Please, Krystar!" I begged you, stop!
"Let's laugh," I cried.

"I'd rather weep and own His chair
Than laugh and own
The piteous nothing that I own."
You turned.
"See how powerless we are, Ansond?
Lions, Eagles, Lightning!" you mimicked God!

I still remember how
The new-made men looked down—
Heaven tolerating shame:
But what I most recall
Is that His mighty power
Absorbed your insolence
And still permitted you to live.

Think of it!
He sometimes tolerates our petty petulance
As a lion assaulted by a fly
Allows the fly to live,
And yet not merely live
But even dog His power with insolence.

There can only be one reason
He endured your haughty slur!
He loves.
And from that moment on,
He set Himself to win you back.
Oh, this is "grace" before the word was coined!
He might simply have erased your being,
Then started over with another new-made prince.
But because He loves He took the harder way!

Our fellows held their breath
As all the Light of Heaven
Condensed in Spirit arms
That reached out to embrace you.
"Come, Krystar, now and drink of deep warm grace.
Love begs you feel again My firm embrace."

"Give me lions, eagles, lightning!
And I'll accept Your love."
You pushed Him back.

No eagles came! No lions!
"See, Ansond, He alone holds sway,"
You sneered.
"We may laugh with Him, Ansond,
But ours is weaker laughter!—
Mere mourning in disguise.
We are but two small embryos.
He is the only proud adult in all of Heaven!
He made us weak to be kept weak—
The playthings of a Father-Tyrant

Who sees His sons as toys.
The food we need to make us gods
He keeps on shelves too high for us to reach!
He makes no sons, just marionettes—
String-handed fools like us
Existing to amuse Him."
You stopped and turned
To all the new-made hosts
And cried your blighted case,
"Lament your being!
You, too, were made for pity.
Here is your blighted, universal fare.
Poor insect gods! Behold Him and despair.
His laughter's power! His power, a tyrant's chair!"

Sin: spending all life's silver choices
To buy a destiny of lead.
How often I've seen men
Cast dollars
In a beggar's cup,
While inwardly they wished
That they could play
His old accordion.
Thus they walked on through the rain
As envy canceled out their alms.

IX

That's how it was that day, Krystar.
Your speech created restlessness in heaven!
Among the tens of thousands of new men
Were Brenn and Daysun, who seemed
To hurry to your cause and make it theirs.
"Father-Spirit, may we also choose?" cried Brenn.
"For choice alone allows us to be men!"

"What would you choose, if choice were yours?"

"I would choose love," cried Brenn.

"I, power," Daysun said.

Again there came a restlessness,
One-hundred-thousand times one-hundred-thousand
Beings shuffled on their feet
In madding indecision and unrest.
Some choosing power
And some desiring love.
Some choosing in confusion not to choose.
Our Father-Spirit groaned,
"Choose power or love,
But know, that choice is both
The gift and burden of each day.
Choice is the heavy weight of God.
It is the sacrifice, the holocaust
Which damns the future
In the moment it decides.
Choose, therefore, carefully—
In laughter after song!
Choose only when your heart is glad.
For if you choose amidst the sweltering of grudge
Lust will occupy the place of love
And power with muddy boots will
Stomp all unborn time in its disdain.
Choose slowly, wisely . . . only after prayer.

Choose when your heart has taught itself to care.
Let choice rise in clean, clear silence
Not when the heart is filled with noise.
Or when the voices of advice congest your reason.

"Choose when your eyes are washed by tears
And your inmost soul can hear
The whispers of other ages—other worlds!

"But choose you must,
For choosing is the meat and drink
Of time and history.
Decision nominates all being.
To decide is to become!
Those who cannot choose
Are prisoners to time.
Those who won't decide are slaves!

"Live not too short a while
Nor yet too long a time in indecision.
Impulsiveness gives life away
In rapid handfuls
But soon despises all its instant generosity.
Yet those who linger long in indecision
Use up their years in peacelessness
And live to envy those
Who risked themselves in swifter choice.

"Never choose what—at the time of choice—
You know is evil.
For you by such an act
Make evil not an outward counselor
But inward fiend.

"Therefore, choose good and live!
At night make every star your counsel.
By day stand in the sun to choose.
Choose good and destiny will be a friend.
Choose evil and destroy what might have been."

A saint at prayer
Is wrapped in such adoring fire
He shames
The shallow flames
Of bridal nights
Where ardent paramours
Seek only for themselves
Yet overnobly name their union love.

X

Come, Krystar, Ansond, come,"
The Father-Spirit called to us.
"I give you both the gift of will.
Have what you will, be free!"

"I am content!" I laughed.

"What, nothing more! Cry lions, eagles, lightning
And behold what gifts are yours!"
The Father-Spirit urged.

"Shall all these things be made by my weak word?"
I was puzzled.

"By your *strong* word they shall."

"If I can make them be
By calling out their names
I see no need to prove it to myself.
I am content to trust!"

"What," cried the Father-Spirit,
"Is peace so great a gift?"

"Yes, Father, yes, all that I crave
Is gilded in the stuff of peace.
Peace is all. It is unbegotten lust.
It is free laughter and untroubled rest.
It smiles in darkness,
Roots itself in safety.
It snuggles into alien arms
And trusts the cabled bridge
To span the crevasses of doubt.
Peace measures every wind
And orders it to be a breeze.
Peace stares down lightning
And bids the thunder be a lullaby

To help the children sleep.
Peace treasures all adversity
And reaches out to pain
That it may touch the world's despair with healing.
Peace cuts up boots of war
And sews them into dancing shoes.
It stops the hearse and cries,
'Oh, be not dead but live with us.'
Peace sleeps within the center of the winds
So calm can fill the sails
And set the course that life should take.
Give me peace. It is Your finest gift.
It is the cradle of Your soul, O God!"

"Then you want nothing more?"
Our Father-Spirit cried.

"One thing I'd own besides this peace!
I want my separateness
To enter into union with Yourself!
I crave to enter You, my God,
And dwell inside the richness of Your being.
Give me no power lest I discover lust.
Rather, give me of Your gracious self
And wait with me while worlds are born or time
        decays.
Make me rich by asking me to risk myself.
Order me to peril for Your name's sake.
Make me a martyr in whatever fire will honor You.
I want to know You in Your mysterious hiddenness.
And thrill to ride the storms with You.
And if You hide from me,
I'll fly into the fiery heart
Of new made stars to seek You there.
I'll chase Your fleet and fleeing presence
Into the cold extremes of every cosmic darkness.
I'll find You in caves and caverns
Of Your flight.

I'll dive into the deep abyss
And feel my way along the halls of nothingness
Until I grapple, yes and grasp
And fold You into my needy soul.
Hold me in the center of Your laughter
Till I am lost unto myself.
Then, if You would give me all I ask,
I beg You to erase the separating seam
That makes us two
Till we are merged in hidden inwardness!"

I stopped my rhapsody of need.
My words seemed small,
And yet the new-made hosts fell down
And wept at them!
I felt ashamed!
"Earthmaker, come! Dissolve all I may be.
Fold littleness into immensity!"

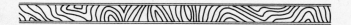

From a mind, light-years wide, came men.
From narrower minds came soldiers forth.
From soldiers, wars
From wars,
Decaying silence.
What hope can our earth hold of peace?
For battlefields came first in Heaven.

XI

I 'm sure you stand these days
And never take your hand
From off the hilt of your great sword.
You made the sword
The day He denied you power.
I think so often of that day
I came upon you working at the crystal forge.
You hammered on the silver steel
Till you had honed
A double edge for your great blade.
I asked you what it was and why you'd made it.
You said that it would serve you well.
That you could use it any time you needed it.
You told me I must wait to see.
The dark foreboding of your sword
Imperiled Heaven.

The same day I chose love alone,
Our Father-Spirit spoke to you,
"Krystar, yours too is choice,
Choose what you will!"
You straightened and smiled.
Your entire being brightened!
You touched the hilt of your new sword.
Your dull face broke into a leer
Then tightened to a grin.
"I choose not peace or folded inwardness,
I choose to have . . . to own . . .
To make the world around me tremble!
Lions, eagles, lightning!" you shouted.

"Then may it be," the Father cried.

Two lions leapt from nothingness
And circled all your glowing joy
And you were pleased.

Eagles too appeared as distant specks
Of brown that grew in size and screamed,
Shattering serenity and diving,
Talons downward until they clawed
The thick glass filament of light.
Tongued lightning
Forked in blinding blue and white
Then fell about your very shoulders.
The spellbound host was awed!
"See what I have made—
Rich presents for myself—
Laugh . . . Laugh at power!"

And so they laughed at your command!
But, Krystar, you were the first
To cease your laughter.
You looked at once morose!
"My laughter all too soon grows empty,
I must make more to laugh more."

"More eagles!" you cried.
They came and fluttered downward.
"More lions, too!"
You stood at last
Amidst a great menagerie of life.

Your greed staunched all your laughter.
You were a grim, ungrinning god,
Hard-faced and empty in your breast!
"Father-Spirit, I find too little joy
In merely calling things to be.
There is one other thing
I yet must have to laugh.
I want a second towering chair."

The Father-Spirit reached in love
To touch you, Krystar.
You recoiled!

"Has all this host that you have made
The power to choose as I?" you asked our Father.

"All have the right of choice, Krystar."

You thought for only a moment
Before you blurted out,
"I will that all of those whom I behold
Should have no will but mine!"

"That I cannot give!
You may not choose to take their will,
For freedom is My greatest gift.
Anyone may sell his gift
Or give it to another
But none may have it taken from him.
Krystar, desist! Be wise!"

"Give me a throne of glass
Or make no pretense of Your love,
While You hold all the power."

"Come, son Celeste, let's celebrate!
Seek peace, not power!
Power eats the eyes of dreams
Then leaves the vision black
And dreamers blind."

Krystar, your face was stone.
You suddenly seized that new-made sword
And thrust your glass-forged blade
Into a lion you so lately made.
Thus murder struck at savage dignity.
The sword flashed silver blood
Into a world that never had seen dying.
A chilling wind blew through
The halls of our high realm.
The dying lion roared, then whispered out of voice.
Nobility, cold-slain by evil choice.

The greatest lie
And most defiling curse
Is that which grins
And spoils the universe.

XII

You left and took the sword with you.
So many of our brothers followed you,
Hordes of proud defiant troops—
Far too many to be counted.

Time crept like slime
Along the unspoiled boulevards
Of a city waiting for your host to pass.
We knew when next we saw you
Each of those who followed you
Would have a sword like yours.

The air bore heavy moans
Like thunder at a distance.
"Father, there is a strange and alien howling
Hovering above the Plains of Light,"
I said.

"It is the sound of hate," our Father-Spirit sighed.
"Your brother's heart seethes as a caldron of his
          grudge.
Go to him, Ansond, and beg him come again to me,
To this fair place."

"Where is he, Father-Spirit?"

"Where dark is thickest . . .
Where the gloom clots
And black despair falls weeping
Into emptiness.
Where roaring sets her tremors
Gnawing hope's unsure foundations."

"Can I call back my power-mad brother?
Has his hate grown hopeless, Father-Spirit?"

"No, only death is hopeless . . .
Go, bring your brother back, but,

Do not look upon his face,
For howling spite has changed it."

I walked to the edge of light.
I knew, Krystar, your standing place
Was in the starless darkness.
I would obey my Father.
Though I despised the darkness,
His commission unto me
Would not be carried out in fear.

"Never fear the night, son Ansond,
Mark now how easily the dark is broken.
Let there be light!"

Like rotted cloth, the black sky tore
Itself in blinding, searing light—
Ripping outward from the Plains of Light.
In the new clean light
My courage was restored.

"Are you afraid, Ansond?" our Father probed.

"Afraid . . . to bid my double-sculpted twin come
      home?"

"Go then.
But mark your zeal with readiness
For when you meet your brother,
He will not seem your twin.
Still, his form can never turn away my need
To call my lost son home again.
I love this child whose grudge is deep as bone!
Oh, hurry, son, and bring your brother home!"

At His word, I flew in search of you.
However far His light extended
The darkness seemed to outrun it,

Yet somewhere at its blacksome heart
I knew that you would dwell.
Down, down through hellish night
I hurried seeking you
Until the howling grew intense.

At last I came before your dingy court.
I remember seeing all the swords
Glinting there like lions dying in the night.
I felt awe-hushed by the dark-hulked spectres,
Crouching fiends in unbegotten darkness.

"How many have joined you?"
I asked.

"Ten thousand times ten thousand,"
You replied.

"Have you enough?"

"Enough," you said. How sure you were!
Your confidence itself seemed evil.
"The war will not last long.
We'll storm the throne and . . ."

"I beg you no!" I cried.

You nearly shouted in reply!
"I will own that crystal chair,
Where sits our infirm, aging parent
Who shall regret His choice
Of giving me no power."

"Can your darkness overcome His light?" I asked.

"Light hurts our eyes, makes ashes of our bones
But we will cope with light and storm His throne."

"Krystar, do you hate our Father?" I asked.

"With every fiber of my being."

"Can you yet call eagles
From the empty sky and lions out of nothingness?"

"Of course," you said.
Your lips grew leathery and firm.

You lied! I see it now.
Your boasts were empty.
Still, I begged you to do it, if you could.

But you declined,
"Not now, but when the battle shall be roused
I shall unleash a storm where love is housed."

Worlds are sculpted in a moment
If the chisel's large enough!

XIII

While we argued over your assault
On the empire of His glory
Our Father was fashioning new hope.

Down into the middle of a deep unplaneted sea
Where light and ebbing darkness swirled and sepa-
     rated
Our Father hurled a brand new world.
Brenn our brother, watched the new and distant world
Move from silent floating
To a slow and growing spin
Which furnished this blue orb
With night and day and seasons urging years.

Brenn was intrigued
And asked our Father-Spirit,
"Why, when war is stirring
In these plains of light,
Do we gaze upon one planet
In the night?"

"Heaven is not the only place of hope,"
Replied the Father-Spirit.
"This little ball holds possibilities
That love may grow in all arenas
To rise from souls quite different
From any that we have ever seen."

Brenn nodded, but said nothing.

That's how it was.
A world was born there in a moment:
In the twinkling of our Father's eye!
It was a world for incubating
God-sized dreams.

Krystar, as the final hour comes close
And you raise the banner to begin

Remember that the sand is almost through the glass
And even though you risk your soul
Your battle will be so intense
That this planet which He made so easily
Will be once more the point of your defeat.

You've been beaten back so often
But of all of your losses
Three of them stand out.
The two women,
Remember whom you met as mothers and as queens,
They were but opportunities to you!

First came Earth's first-made woman,
Queen of the beginnings.
You seduced her, stinging her to impure conscience.
Rape knows one form more brutal
Than that which tears at flesh.
Seduction is the word that ravages
All loyalty, fidelity, and worship.
You turned the woman from two other lovers:
Her Father, who doted on her simple prayers.
And her man, who blessed
Each sunrise while they lived together.
The fruit of folly was your gilded lie.
She reached for it
And tasted it and
Felt the thrilling shame of first betrayal.
She thought the taste was sweet
Until its nectar of narcissism
Distilled to wormwood
And poisoned all her destiny.

But the maid who gave the world God's Son,
Was not so easily seduced—
Remember how she bore the
Lord of Heaven in her very womb
While all the time you sought

To turn her from her purposes.
She beat you in her merely human strength
Made strong by the devotion
Unto Him she mothered.

The final time you were defeated
By her Son and our glorious Father
Who formed the earth to be the hope!
Do you recall that day?
The woman's Son hung on Terra dying . . . slowly . . .
    slowly. . .
You hurled insults and He wept
At the severity of human sin
That held Him to wood.
You danced above His grave
And howled above His deadness
And celebrated your supposed victory.

But you were beaten even then
Before you started.
Did you actually think
That God would leave Him dead?
Poor Krystar!
He breathed again, then stood!
His first breath brought a white-hot revolution.
Of such power the world itself
Could laugh away the heavy centuries.
His dying earthquake shook the tombs
And crying life rose powerfully
To plate the stars with gold.
The life with which he conquered
Was victory for Him not you.

Now, brother,
I am still amazed at your naïveté.
You cannot win against our Sovereign!
He will win this final war!
It grieves me I must fight with you on His behalf!

I dread the final battles of Heaven's civil conflict.
I love you but love shall not forestall my will to win.
I do intend to stop your pillage of His universe.

When you have lost,
Let all your greed remember
How He begged you not revolt.
He loved His blue-green Terra!
It was to be His special world of unspoiled hope.
Now it's but a battleground!

Oh, that you had played life differently!
Oh, that you had come home to love!
Love holds the power of change when souls confess
And demons are transformed by brokenness.

When God makes love a drama
His theater is all the universe:
His audience, a single broken heart.

XIV

Heaven wears the heavy garment doulet?," cried
  our Father,
"Come and let's put on the lighter robe of hope
And bless the night of heaven's pain.
Be, Terra, be!
Fly, bold world, fly!
Between the sunny light and starless night.
Never fear the cold of empty space.
You shall not fly against this midnight
Without some certainty.
Dark space be lit with suns,
Born by the thousands,
To fill this emptiness."

No sooner had He spoken, than the night splintered
  into
Flecks of brilliance and super novae brighter even
Than those thousand, thousand suns
Broke into being!
Music played.
The spheres agreed to His command of life.
Worlds unnumbered heard the music.

"I cannot be content to love so narrowly
One Realm of Light. A growing universe
Is barely room enough to fill My hungry need.
Come laughter.
Come music!
Come life!
When My son, Krystar, sees these new dimensions
Of exploding love, he will return!
Then he will choose life!
For he will see the glory of it!
Death will seem so small
When he considers life
And when he sees life grow

And then inhabit all the galaxies.
He will come back to truth.
He'll see that hate, in clinging to its littleness,
Can only shrink and dwindle.
Embarrassed that it ever was.
I wait for you, Krystar.
This joyous planet is your resting place—
Oasis begging rebels 'drink of Grace.'"

It's hearts, not faces, that make
Twins identical.

XV

So Terra came to be while I begged you
To come back to our Father.
There was time then.
The world was new,
Your revolution undeclared.

When finally we met
I had some trouble in remembering
That we were twins.
For our choosing had left us most unalike.
I trembled, Krystar, to see you had become
A fanged and rasping soul.
You greeted me by sneering out your evil envy.
"Ansond, I see you have not changed.
Why not?—Love bears a boring beauty."

I ignored your confrontation.
"I've come to take you home," I pled.
"Our Father wants you back even as you are."

"To be His vassal?"

"To be His laughter once again!"

"I will not laugh till I have all I want!"

"A throne above His own?" I asked.

You , glaring, answered nothing.
I still can see the steely hardness
In your fierce bronze eyes.

"But would you really find any joy
In seeing our Father-Spirit grovel at your feet?"

At the word "feet," I saw you lower claws,
Recoiling inwardly at your degeneration.
"Come home, please," I begged.

You nodded to two monstrous fiends
Who drug me to a stake and chained me.
"Ansond, don't wince," you spat.
"I merely offer you
What you've already chosen for yourself . . . slavery!"

Your words were overwhelming.
"Bind him now," you cried.
Your large foundlings fettered me in irons.
"Here, Ansond, at the stake of choice
You must decide!
Choose broader than you have!
Those who choose both light and darkness
Understand the whole world."

"No! Instead, I beg you to choose narrower.
Consider what your broadened evil choice has cost.
See how you've changed,"
I paused and shuddered and went on,
"Lest I should be like you—
I will not choose at all."

"Then let this trial begin."
Your words were all it took.
Two others brought a swinging pot
Of fuming incense passing it
Beneath my swimming consciousness.
Its too sweet odors drugged my senses
Till my chains and stake gave way
To pleasant visions.

I wore a crown!
My throne was all of golden glass
And rose above the Realm of Light.
My own great chair towered far above our Father's.
I felt a vast exhilaration.
I stood and raised my scepter.
Like God, Himself, an emperor,

And drunk with power, I laughed
Until I looked down at my hand
Which grasped the mace of office.
The hand in which I held the scepter
Had become a lizard's claw!

"No!" I cried.
"My cry devoured your poisoned vision.
I woke and staring downward
Past my poor chained arms
Saw with some relief
My hands and feet were still my own—
Not claws at all."

"Come, Ansond, drink again!"
You smirked.

A second time Daysun brought in the sweet incense.
The odor lifted me above the Plains of Light.
I flew while crying, "Lions, eagles, lightning!"
And below me on the shelf of glass
Rose powerful beasts
That stood in feral power
And eagles at my trumpet words
Circled through great thunderheads of light.

I landed in their midst
And fear with fangs tore at my face.
The lions lengthened into snakes
Slithering around my body
In thick and crushing coils.

"No!" I cried. "Free me, Krystar!"

A final time you called for Daysun
Who passed the sweetness past my face.
This time, I held a long red sword.
I flew on wings of power

Throughout the length of heaven.
I flew, at last, to that great throne and hurled my
    blade
Into the silent waiting chair.
Steel slaughtered Spirit!
The blood of God flowed out among the stars.
I wept at my foul crime.
The vision numbed like some narcotic
And I slept in stench and stupor.

When I awoke, your spell was done.
My wrists were bound and yet my heart was free.
Love held as power reached out enticingly.

Heaven loves the few who doubt
More than she loves all those
Who never cared enough to question.

XVI

While we argued over your assault
On the empire of His glory
Our Father was fashioning new hope.

Down into the middle of a deep unplaneted sea
Where light and ebbing darkness swirled and sepa-
          rated
Our Father hurled a brand new world.
Brenn our brother, watched the new and distant world
Move from silent floating
To a slow and growing spin
Which furnished this blue orb
With night and day and seasons urging years.

Brenn was intrigued
And asked our Father-Spirit,
"Why, when war is stirring
In these plains of light,
Do we gaze upon one planet
In the night?"

"Heaven is not the only place of hope,"
Replied the Father-Spirit.
"This little ball holds possibilities
That love may grow in all arenas
To rise from souls quite different
From any that we have ever seen."

Brenn nodded, but said nothing.

That's how it was.
A world was born there in a moment:
In the twinkling of our Father's eye!
It was a world for incubating
God-sized dreams.

Krystar, as the final hour comes close
And you raise the banner to begin

"Come home to love, Krystar,"
I begged and fell a final time.
I lay unconscious underneath the leering
Forms around me.

Then through the bitter circle
Of your huge and hating fiends
Another form walked to me
And lifted me from off the floor.
"Come, Ansond, I'll help you home!"

It was Brenn!
He'd come to take me back.

"I bear two messages to you, Krystar,"
Brenn roared.
"Your beloved Father-Spirit
Reminds you that your thirst for power is vain.
He says that there will always be
A single throne in Heaven,
And yet He begs you to come home to Him."

You paused, then shouted,
"Never . . . lions, eagles, lightning!"

None came.

I stirred at last from my unconsciousness,
"Father-Spirit, I love You . . . Deliver me."

Instantly salvation came.
The sky was darkened by a bird so large,
That even you, Krystar, flinched in terror.

"Why can I not make eagles
Just as you do, Ansond?"
Your question seemed so small and to be pitied.
For a moment your horrible defiance was all gone.

You were a child again.
Our innocence was welded—we seemed those
    brothers
We had been at first.

"Call in love, Krystar," I said, "And everything you
    order
Will come to be. Love alone may order worlds to be.
Hate cannot create."
I and our Father's messenger then mounted on the
    eagle.
We rose and fled the discord of your court.

You shouted upward as we flew,
"What's the second message
From the glass throne?"

"He wants you to know that even now
He is creating
A universe so big that it may hold
The farthest reaches of a love grown bold."

Heaven only once put on the boots of war,
And then because it woke to find the
Enemy inside its gates!

XVII

Entreaty is of little use!
Your brother's firm in his resolve.
The die is cast!
Strife is coming
To the Realm of Light,"
The Father-Spirit sighed.

"Hate war, but never hate your foe.
Hold no spite,
Allow yourself no enemies.
Even when your enemies take arms
And thrust at you with death,
Answer them with life.
Death cannot inhabit this fair place.
This war of angels, I decree, will be
A battle with no fallen.
No killing shall inhabit Heaven!
We shall respond in life
To all of hate's onslaughts.
We'll push Krystar's advancing horde
Beyond the gates of light
To practice evil choices in an evil night."

"Beyond this realm, may they choose love?"
Brenn seemed to seek in hope.

"Always and, of course, they may choose love!
But hate is all-too-soon made prisoner to habit.
And habit, with long practice
Becomes itself a chain
So ponderous it drags the heart
Toward an icy bitter grave
With everlasting grudges.
Krystar, my own . . . my love . . . my joy!
You are forever lost to me!"

Silence followed . . . sobbing too.
Not weak or sickly tears
But crying as a King cries.
The Throne of Heaven shook!
"He is lost whom I hoped to hold forever.
My child, my boy, my son!
This day all hope is swallowed up in grief.
My cherished son is murderer and thief."

Who are you, great Andromeda?
And who made all your flaming suns?
The galaxy took voice and said,
"Ask any furry shrew on earth
Whose tiny heart beats out his worth
And you will find us both quite small
Compared to Him who made us all."

XVIII

A grieving God
Lays by His pain in time
And before the war began
He called to us out of a bright new joy!
"Come, Ansond, Brenn, Gallan,
And fly with me to Terra."
His laughter filled the court
As welcome, warming mirth.

"Come see what I have made,
I call it nature.
A garden for my Godhood!"
He laughed again,
And it was good to hear God's laughter.

"Nature?" asked Brenn. "What is this nature?"

"Nature is a kind of soil
Where wonder may take root in life.
It is life, concerned about its future.
Reproducing, breathing and expanding.
Growing like the green of leaves
And the pink of flesh,
The silver and gold of fin and scale.
Nature is fur and fang and flower:
Feather and typhoon—wind and wave
And sound, light and ice and fire
Thunder, dawn, and night.
Nature is asteroids swimming in their unseen night
Light years from any eye.
It is some things waiting to be born
And some things dying that they may be.
Nature is the force of all that lives.
It is gravity bending orbits in grand ellipse
Around a thousand, thousand unnamed suns.
It is infant animals sucking out their mother's life

That these they nourish will in time
Supply their own milk to their kind and die.

"All Humankind shall be the highest crown of
        nature.
Still, it is Humankind who,
In arrogance of ego,
They'll learn a few of my great laws
And name them for themselves
To call my vast predictability
By little, mortal names.

"They will see through only surface layers of nature
And name their sutured surgery their Science.
But no matter, Science can but name
What nature will at last completely swallow:
Nature shall elude
Their best attempts to fully understand it.
Nature is all there is one realm separate from Heaven.
Come fly with me, behold it for yourself."

The Father-Spirit flew ahead of us
And so we followed Him on Spirit wings.
We soared past forming planets
And starscapes in collapse,
Past sluggish quasars,
And forming nebulae
And graying galaxies of gas-ringed worlds.
Until at length we settled
Downward to a blue-green ball
Shrouded white by clouds and mists.
We walked in ten-league strides
Past red-rimmed canyons
And green-edged lakes

In this splendid world made new and gold
And green and brown

We four, at last, sat down beside a stream
That spilled in rippling laughter over rocks.
Small living things stared back at us,
Some chattered and some chirped.
Some flew in feathered softness
From glistening underbrush.
A tiny ball of fur with molten eyes
Peered out at us with eyes of drunken wonder,
Then scampered through a bush
To stop and stare once more
And then move on.

I laughed with such a volume
That the shallow cliffs
Before the distant mountains
Seemed drawn to laugh with me.
"Did you make all these tiny things?" I asked.

"At once," the Father-Spirit answered.
"Laugh, please, then laugh again, son Ansond,
This world is myriad and amplifies
The joys that we pass by
Inside our shining Realm of Light."

"How myriad is nature?" asked Brenn.

"You cannot imagine all of it,"
The Father-Spirit exulted.
"For I have hidden tiny flowers
In mountain crags where
None will ever see them.
They will bloom
For no eyes other than my own,
And then these tiny unseen blooms
Will fade, begetting others of their kind.

"In the deepest ocean floor
Are eyeless, living denizens

Whose brilliancy is lost in depth
Too dark for any eyes—
Yet more and thousands more
Are born each time we laugh.
A single syllable of mine
Breaks into breezes calling out
For life, and with each summons more species come
      to be."

He now talked low,
In a kind of low, sweet melody
That made the life forms swell in number
Till whirring in warm grass and
Chirping in the leafy forests
They burrowed in earth,
As lofty soaring life then came:
High on silver, unseen wires, suspended
Until at last His spectacle was ended.

Twinkle, twinkle, galaxy.
Whence came your luminosity?
Was it from astronomy
Or from your own autonomy?
Ah . . . Ah . . . Ah . . . We will have
    honesty!

XIX

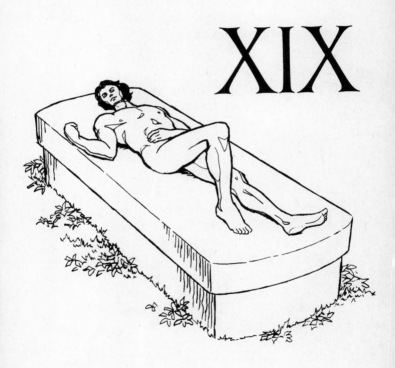

When we returned from Terra
Brenn and Gallan seemed to grow remote.
They walked away from those
Who kept the central place around the chair.
Who can say why?
And yet it seemed to me
That angels grown remote are soon to be
Allied with Hell and evil villainy.
I knew they would defect!
Your revolution grew in strength each day,
More and more of our realm defected
To your swelling insurrection.

Like all your hordes, Krystar,
Brenn and Gallan were among those
Who once stood with us at the high glass chair.
But they were choosing even now
To leave our Father
And bear His glorious secret to the enemy.
What offering could they bear?
They knew of Terra!
They had touched down upon her crust,
And walked her lands and knew her rivers.
I discovered their whole scheme,
And quite by happenstance!
I followed them one bright morning
Until they'd reached our realm's edge.
They plunged over and repeated that same flight
We'd flown before . . . I followed them . . . to Terra.
They felt my presence in pursuit
And all of us landed at that stream
Where the forest formerly had made a place for us.

"Ansond," Brenn spoke first,
"Here we are on this fair world again.
Why do you think He made it?"

"It is a place where, as He said,
He can create in newness
And where life unknown before
Can be created as He will."

"I keep thinking," said Gallan,
"That this might be a pretty place
For Krystar to bed down,
If he should lose his crystal place.
It's not so roomy as our realm
And the light is not so bright.
Still, there's a pleasantness about the place.
It could well be a place to live.
Do you think He would permit it?"

"No," I said, "No more than
He'd give any kind of evil,
A place within His realm."

"Still did He not say," asked Brenn,
"That those new creatures He'd create
Could choose their own sovereignty?
Suppose they'd choose Krystar
And not our Father-Spirit?"

"Yes . . . suppose," said Gallan.

"It's quiet here," said Brenn.

"We know the way, too!" said Gallan.
I could tell by listening,
They would not long be of us.
I left them there, returning to our Father.

I knew, Krystar, that they would
Offer you allegiance.
I knew these two trustees of secrets
Would tell you in their time

All that you'd need to know
To spoil every world.
There's such contagion in iniquity.
It spreads like fire through every galaxy.

Following that experience,
I felt a season of impending melancholy
Until our Father-Spirit spoke to me
And called me to accompany Him
On yet another journey
To His brand new world.
"Come, Ansond, I am working on a masterpiece."

Following the wind of Spirit
We came at last to a clearing
Where a slab of stone
Was raised like an artist's table.
On it lay a body, small but naked,
Not powerful like ourselves,
But beautiful in form.

"Man." The Father-Spirit smiled.
"He too can choose."

"Then he will have the gift of will?"

"He, like you, may choose to hate or love.
In many ways he is like
All creatures that comprise his world.
He, like them, is hair and flesh,
Bone and claw.
But, unlike them, by simple will,
He has the grace to be like us,
Both in kind and quality of life."

"And all this world will be his realm?"
        I asked.

"All of Terra will be his!
But best of all, the hate that scarred our realm
Never can come here . . . unless . . .
This human makes the choice to hate."

"And if he does choose hate?"

"His realm though loved is transient,
Nature bears a weakness
Unfound in our fair place.
Terra will decay in time
Should he choose hate.
Death could come to this small world.
And savage wars, where nature spoils itself.
The burden of this heavy choice must all be his!"

We stared down at his sleeping form.
"When will he live?" I asked.

"When I breath over him
And fill his soul
With all My purposes and hopes.
His time is soon, but not yet."

A beautiful snake slithered past our feet.
I shuddered, spasm-bound to fear
And felt night-coldness in the atmosphere.

I met a man who kept two heads,
And thus he really kept two minds.
His heads fell into quarreling
And bit each other very blind.
He died a month thereafter.
Where teeth and bloody faces fought.
So all duplicity brings death
In quarreling, doubled thought.

This letter's near complete,
I'll finish it for soon we must
Leave gentler causes
And prepare to finish up this war
Begun so long ago.

Remember now—back past these human years?
All day you gathered up your troops
Upon the battleground of light.
Soldier fiends with silver swords
Determined hate would win.
Armies of your thousands,
And ten thousand times ten thousand,
Cosmic as the forming galaxies
That spun away in quasars from
The dingy fields of your dread war.

Along a battle front light-years in width
Glass fire rang out upon glass fire
And flame on flame.
Fatigue, not death, became our only enemy.
Our Father had decreed
Our war would be a war
Where none could die.
Those who might have died
Fell to sleeping when stabbed
By the kind weapons of our war.
Thus as our flaming swords
Fell in opened, silver lesions,
Every wound was healed,
Even as the blade withdrew.
Thus all of your evil forces
Fell into sleeping heaps
Slain by the coma we inflicted.

Always in the fierceness of the fray,
Your armies trained in dark

Were overwhelmed by light.
Your legions limped before our bright pursuers.
You were pushed back inch by inch,
Drawing ever nearer to that threshold
Where the Realm of Light was ended
And the Night of Space began.
Gallan, your general, could hear the ringing
Blows of hate and war, but
Had no taste for war.
He seemed to be your only undecided soldier
Who did not clearly opt for
The destiny he'd chosen.
Power, he knew, had been his evil choice.
He had no avid need to gain your dream
And rule from his glass chair.
Rather, he often thought of Terra
As it hung pristine in new framed space.
It seemed a great oasis in the midst of holocaust.

He was lost in thought
And wishing he might be there
When Brenn passed him.
Brenn had come
To clear aside your wounded, sleeping
Knights of darkness, paralyzed by war.
"Not fighting, Gallan?" called Brenn.
Reluctantly, Gallan gathered up his
Shield and sword and moved toward the battle line.

He thought again of nature and of Terra—
That new-made world where love would never cease
And yet a perfect place for war or peace.

No sooner did a dark knight fall,
Than we would pick them up and carry them
To the edge of space to hurl their sleeping bodies
From the shelf that marked the shining limits
Of your waning war.

Paralyzed from battle wounds
Each sleeping denizen floated from
The shelf out to the void beyond.
Away—so silently—away
Leaving darksome space an army's quiet grave.

The War of Light raged on.
In the mayhem of the battle
You slipped the lines
And moved toward the high glass throne
Until a single soldier barred your way.

"Gallan!" you cried!

Gallan felt a sudden fear—
His heart was still quite undecided
On his loyalty to our Father's cause.
He had come most late to side with treachery
And yet he struggled to undecide
His unsure decisions.

"Wretched soul am I!" he cried.
"Choosing, choosing—each unsettled day
I make a choice, yet choice is in my way!"

"Gallan," you cried again, Krystar!
"Leave the Realm of Light
And serve with me
Or here and now I'll take your life
And you will pay for your betrayal."

"Die! It is impossible!
The King of Light says dying cannot be.
In all this realm—only life is here!"

Still, Gallan eyed your blade and trembled . . .
And dropped his sword.
It clattered on the glass pavement

Creating terror in his heart.
Then, Krystar, you swung your blade!
It cut the air above him
With a singing sound.
"Please, no!" Gallan begged.

"Why should I spare you!"
Gallan winced and spoke with halting words.
He hated to betray the lovely planet
That had of late consumed his dreams.
To tell or not to tell was his betraying issue.
Gallan stood wondering and doubting
Till you screamed at him again, "Why?"

"Because I know of something that could
Benefit your hordes and give your dying fiends
A chance to live again.
I know a small uncharted world
That you might find
A safe retreat, Lord Krystar.
It is more beautiful than you could ever know.
It is crammed with what our Father-Spirit
Has named nature,
And nature is unspoiled beauty."

"Why should I care that
Such a world exists?"

"Because, Krystar,
Your war must fail;
You know you cannot win.
And when it's over,
You will know only outer darkness."

You snarled over Gallan's words,
But he went on!
"But when this war is lost,
I'll guide you there and you can live

And gather up ourselves again for future
Wars till your almighty grudge
May prove, at last, triumphant over God.
On His new planet, Terra,
You will have the home you longed for.
A chair as high as you might raise.
A place to be a Prince, if not a King."

"Then show me . . . give me!"

But Gallan clenched his lips
In steel resolve!
One of the warriors near
Smashed his mailed fist into the traitor's face.
"Tell Lord Krystar the name and way
To this new place,"
The killing fiend demanded.
Gallan uttered only one word, "Terra—"
Before he fell unconscious in his heavy chains.
And even as he slept
Hot tears poured from his clenched eyes.
Paralysis stops everything but crying.
A coma shuts the eyes, yet tears flow free
When inwardness is vised in treachery.

I only thrill at Redwoods
When I have eaten and am filled.
I cry how very lovely,
Oh, Poetry, please come!
But in interludes of hunger
I prefer a bush with plums.

XXI

When the war was all but over
The Father-Spirit and I flew again
Past worlds half-formed . . . past infant suns
Till the shadows of existence
Fell into shadowed pristine innocence.

We came a final time to the
Blue-green glow of Terra
And passed its sunny fields,
Its blue majestic mountains,
Veiled waterfalls and
Swirling green cascades until
We came to that high-vaulted dome of
Soaring trees where we earlier had walked.

The woods were strangely silent
As though the simple act we
Came to do would
Hush the entire universe.
I walked up to the silent slab
To see the Father-Spirit's newly sculpted,
Finished, waiting man.

The Father-Spirit looked wistfully
Into the distant green
And lifted up his head and sang
An anthem to the sleeping man.

"Walk slowly, gently, on the waiting earth
Ordering each step lest it should run
Past light and miss the golden earth
Or sunny fields or wonders unbegun.

"Walk peaceably and hushed by the great within.
Make soundless songs your final inwardness,
For song is light and noise but spins
A web of dark where certainty must guess.

"Learn, reaching up, to stretch the heart toward God.
Learn, reaching down for treasures in the dust.
One hand may touch the sky and from the sod
Your sullied fingers feel an earthen trust.

"Make living rich with risk. Despise safe course—
Walk fearlessly where none has laid a trail.
"Smile at the threat of thunder's cosmic force.
Touch wind, chase fire then reach to catch the gales.

"Stare at the sky till pain afflicts the eye.
Train vision lest it dart from place to place.
For glancing harries sight—bids vision die,
Has sight, yet cannot see the Father's face.

"Let no impatient hour be ever lost
Nor fail to feel the sun's earthwarming pass.
Hold honey in the mouth and savor frost.
Raise straw to light and celebrate the grass.

"Some rhapsodies elude the human ear.
Some splendid music dies on deaf-mute lips.
Some symphonies you glean by heart in fear.
Some sweet chorales are heard by fingertip!

"Grow manward—yet in wonder stay a child
In need—live free—let but one need cry out:
Love me, love earth, love truth. With undefiled
Commitment, love all that life's about.

"Remain asleep for now, leaf-canopied
By grace! Blue domed by new-made skies,
For soon her coming feet in hurried need
Shall pleat the golden fields with lovers sighs.

"Oh, sleep in joy, your bride and queen comes soon.
Make long your lust to be, for being's length
Will stand encrowned by sun, and stars, and moon
To wake your sleeping soul in passion's strength."

When the song was finished I wept!

My words were weak refrain
To all that He had sung:
"Oh, Terra, Terra—place of man,
You are the Father-Spirit's final dream
Of greatness. This world is proof
That love cannot abide a cruel, unfurnished
      emptiness.
When you awake, remember
You are loved and bear all the responsibility
That here is given you:
Love and choose! It is your destiny!"

From each of two bright silver pouches
I took a single tree
And planted it
On either side of him who slept.
It was a single act of peace
That broke the war of light.
Both saplings, oddly different,
Seemed to know
That in the course of years
They'd grow to towering trees
And that each one would bear
A different kind of fruit.
How fast trees grow
And yet how slow.
A century would change
The saplings into kings.
A quiet thousand years would pass
Before the chirping forest woke
The sculpted man who lay without a voice
Between the infant monarch trees of choice.

Two noble generals who hated war
Agreed upon that narrow commonality
To try to love each other.
Said one, "I have in my homeland a
    family."
"I, too," the other one agreed.
Each showed the other portraits of their
    wives
And then embraced and spared a
    thousand lives!

XXII

Your struggle, Krystar, could not last.
In desperation of your cause
You flew directly to the throne
And reached it at the very moment
I returned from Terra.

We faced each other there the final time.

"Ansond, embrace your brother,"
Our Father-Spirit called to me.

At His word I walked to you and
Threw my arms out to embrace you.
No matter that your former form was gone.
Or that you had become a hideous beast.
You doubled your mailed claw
And threw your scaly arm in such
An arc of power that I
Sprawled backward.

"Krystar," our Father softly pledged,
"Even in your evil form
I would embrace you, had I, like
Ansond, arms that could permit
The glory of embrace.
I would touch you, skin to golden skin
So you would 'feel' the love I bear."

But you ignored His words
And shouted out old grudges.

"Was it so much to give me . . .
A throne beside your own?"

"Krystar . . . Krystar, do you not see?
It was not the throne that I withheld.
I withheld the ravages of your unbridled greed.

No gift is big enough to satisfy
A lover who loves the gift
More than its sacred Giver!"

"But one *small* throne . . ."

Suddenly I saw you as you were.
You were but His ugly child
And you looked piteous,
Made small by greed.
Our Father seemed almost to weep
As He reached out.
"Small thrones want larger thrones.
A little power but languishes in appetite
And where a little power corrupts,
Great power destroys.
See what your lust has caused already . . .
Your brother and your Father, and indeed,
This entire Realm of Song and Laughter
Is pressed beneath the heel of war.
Oh, Krystar, come now
Even at this final moment, and
Forsake your evil lust
And let the three of us embrace
As first we did in laughter.
Ansond, embrace him yet again."

Dutifully, I walked
Without the slightest hesitation and obeyed.
You, draconian brother,
Once more raised your scaly claw
And slammed that fist of hate into my face.
"You cannot kill me
Nor can any hate kill love," I said.
You sneered at me,
Disregarding my torn face.

"But You'll kill me, won't You, Father?"
You were pathetic in your accusation.

"I cannot, and I will not,"
The Father-Spirit said.
"No hate can hold its place
In a universe of love.
If I'd kill you for any reason I'd call noble
I, too, would be a killer.
And even noble killing
Is an impossible step
For the God of life to take.
I give life!
I do not take it!
Come with Me, Krystar."
You followed Him to
The very edge of our Realm.

You both looked out
Above the glittering ballustrade.

"The night is beautiful," the Father-Spirit exulted.
"Out there's a universe unfinished,
Nor will it ever be. It grows!"
It never ceases to expand.
It grows as surely as love grows.
On one small planet near a minor star
That can be seen from here
There rides a dream,
And when the dream is done, I myself,
Will walk upon that little world."

"I've heard about Your world," you sneered!
"But know this, Your world will never live,
For Gallan is in chains and when I leave
This love-ruled sky, he will show me
Your prized planet.
And there I'll have at last the chair
That You denied me!"

"Perhaps, My son, perhaps
But not forever . . .

This universe I've made
Will one day integrate itself and
All will live as one in light
Beneath one throne.
We will meet again, Krystar—My lost joy,
Out there with all our conflicts done . . ."

"Aha . . . Then You will slay me, won't You?
For all Your noble words
Your love, long-stuffed with grudge, will murder me!"

"No . . . never! But out there . . . in a darksome
        corner
Of that glittering night
Is a prison where the very air weeps even now.
It's a hall of errant spirits called
The Canyon of the Damned."

"And You will put me there?"

"No, you will put yourself there,
In choosing hate you chose that cell—
And there you will remain
The victim—of your own corrupted will!
Freedom may choose anything
But it must live with all it chooses.
Every evil choice in time decays
Until its power ebbs into nothingness
And even now your way of death
Neither dies nor lives! It only endures
With heavy hopelessness forever!
Oh, son, beloved
While there is time,
Please cheat the Canyon of the Damned . . ."
Our Father shuddered in His agony.

Then once again He looked at you
And cried to me in tearing, anguished hurt,
'Ansond, embrace My son Krystar."

I walked a final time to you
And opened in embrace to call you
Back into our broken family.
This time, Krystar, you drew your sword
And thrust it through me.
I shuddered then and fell in blood.
The pain was terrible,
Not the pain of bloodshed
But the pain of seeing
Our great Father's love abused!

"Ansond, be not dead."
Our Father cried.

I rose, healed by a silver scar
From your bright, temporary wound!

You threw your sword then at the
very heart of His great chair, crying,
"Love, I despise You
And all that You have made.
I hate this realm and hate Your planet too."

"Krystar, return to Me.
Once outside our realm of love
You never can return.
Call this realm, Light,
And call me Father,
For the time to save yourself
Is short!"

You fled!

I wept!

"Oh, Father, the war is won,
Yet all Your dream is lost.
Power struts before love's weeping last defense.
Must loving worlds be done at such expense?"

They say
That when the war in Heaven ended
God sat a million years
And stared out into space.
"I must never make a man," He wept,
"Unless I create Grace."

XXIII

Y ou were among
The last to leave.
You hurried to the chained Gallan
And drew him to his feet.

"Remove his chains!" you ordered.
Your ugly servants did.

"We are not defeated,
We will come back.
I yet will own this realm and chair,
But not now.
Gallan will show us now
A place to organize our hate."

The fickle Gallan now had scales.
His slitted eyes blinked lizard-like,
And yet there seemed to him
A strange reluctance
To lose the Realm of Light.

"You know the way?"
You asked the traitor.
"I do," he said.

You walked out to the final edge
Of our fair realm.

"We are exiles," you cried.

"But we shall once again storm
These high, glistening gates."
It was an empty boast that
Faded into sky.
The war had ceased!
Your remaining warriors

Leapt into the night
And as they leapt, they wailed,
"Damned . . . Damned! Still, even fiends have
     fiendish dreams
Of crushing worlds in coils of lost esteem."

Prison bars are in the mind alone.
Dungeons are an option of the spirit.

XXIV

Krystar, my brother,
As you lost your war in Heaven,
You soon will lose the battle here on Terra.
The battle lines are drawn.
You know you cannot win,
And now I'll tell you why.
Here is the truth that you have overlooked.
Here is the thing you never understood—
We were not His sons—not really!
Oh, yes, He called us by that name.
It added dignity to all of our existence.
But He had a Son who was Himself . . .
But wait, I hurry the very reason for this letter.
Let me slowly speak all things in better order.

Shortly after you had left the realm,
Our Father called to me!
"Here is the key that bolts
The Canyon of the Damned.
Fly to that wailing house of chains
And open that dank, sunless,
Place where power
That would not turn from lust
Must languish evermore, unsatisfied."
The Father-Spirit gave me a huge key.

I flew the skyway to that
Hidden house of horrors
On the edge of space.
When I returned, the Father-Spirit cried,
"It is finished!"

"But why must there be such a place?"
        I asked.

"Because the universe needs a house
For those who prize power over servanthood,

A place for arrogance to live its half-life.
Still in My loving universe
No house of horrors is permitted long.
No laughter long mocks love."

Oh, brother, the air was close with portent.
A howling broke around me.

Our Father saw your forces
Being pushed forever from our land.
"It has come, Ansond . . .
The end of war . . .
Your brother's leaving.
You alone are now My chief love until—"
He paused!

"Until?" I picked up the hesitation.

"Until . . ." His words stopped again.
"Until Terra!"

"Behold the mystery that is Myself!"

I stared into the center of the chair,
Where the crystal thickened into light,
Whose blue intensity grew bold
Till I shielded both my eyes
Against the brilliance.

And when that brilliance died away
A Youth sat in the center of the chair.
His eyes were lit with that same light
That also filled the chair.

The atmosphere held thunder.
"Here is My Son, Myself."

"Your Son? Yourself?"
My mind reached out.

The seated Youth stood and smiled
And reached His hand
And I reached back,
Till fingertip to fingertip we touched.
Then fingertips slipped over hands
Until the two of us were clasped.
Each held the other's hands.
Face studied face with seriousness
That eased gradually to smiles.

"This," said the Father-Spirit,
"Is the Troubadour—My Singer, and
My Life: My Son, Myself. We two are one!
Inseparable, Invisible, Intangible."
"Intangible?" I asked.
"Not so! We touch!"
The Youth stared through my soul,
And as He did His form diminished,
Faded into air, and then was gone.

"Behold My Son, Myself,
Inseparable, Invisible, Intangible,"
The Father-Spirit said again.

Krystar, here is the nearest truth—the Royal Son!
Here lies the folly of your haughty plan.
You should have worshiped—any being can.
You should have waited till His love made grand
Had stooped to crown His glorious lover, Man!

"Are you two one?" I asked our Father-Spirit.

"We both are one . . . yet three!"

"Oh, yes, Krystar,
We knew of those three Spirits
Crying on primeval winds
As worlds came to be.

What we did not understand
Was that our Father-Spirit's Son
Would enact a drama on the world
He lately made."

Even as the word died on His lips
A flame blazed up inside the chair,
Yet more than flame, it was a roaring fire
That blazed in dancing tongues of light.
And for a moment it seemed
I saw the strong young face
Of the Father-Spirit's Son and Self.
Then every image died.
The fire and Youth were gone.
"Will I ever see Your Son, Your Self again?"
I asked.

"Doubt it not!" The Father-Spirit said.
"You will see and you will hear.
For from this Youth is such a song
That worlds lie forming now within His melodies.
We are one, and one day in His youthful form
I'll walk the dust of Terra.
And in our glorious oneness I'll
Settle once and for all, the struggle of our realm."

A fire blazed in the throne.
The Youth appeared again and lifted up
His bearded head and sang.
At the sheer glory of His song
I wept and breathed His joy.
"Until Terra . . . Until Terra!"

Do you not see, Krystar,
We were not the center of His love.
It seemed that way at first.
It was His Son, Himself—who was the center.
Your arrogance assumed too much!

We, you and I, were but servants of the drama.
We were not the primary players.
The actors were but two.
His Singing Son and Terra's new-made man.
We were there only to serve Him,
We were never meant to be
The sole pursuants of His love.
That was the reason for this letter.
His Realm was for His Son and Him
And all who would later come,
In searching need of God.

Your foolish war was all beside the point.
Heaven's not a plot of earth
Where demons may build castles.
Heaven is relationship.
If you could have defeated him,
Which was not possible, poor soul,
You would not have owned Heaven.
You would have just returned the world to chaos.
In this world there is not love or hate.
It is love or nothing!
It is not peace or war,
It is peace or oblivion.

These truths you never understood.
My letter brings them far too late, I know.

I saw before the first man breathed
That glory soon would come to dust.
The Father's Son
Would soon break into time
Above a forest garden there on Terra.
His song would rip its way
Outward through the stars,
Dancing in celestial ethers.
That song would fly
Through old star systems and infant galaxies

Until it passed a glorious new star,
And settled on the soft blue planet.

Now, brother, you can see it, too,
His music threaded, there
Among the green wax leaves
And twisted as a morning vapor,
Interrupting rainbows.
At last it found a wide green glen
And a broad and gray-white slab of stone.
The melody slid easily upon the sleeping form
That lay there at the sylvan altar.

The sleeping man stood upright.
His being left deep footprints
In the soft new earth of Terra.
Hope was where creation ended, Krystar,
Not with us, but with humankind.
You never stayed quite long enough
In Heaven to know the entire play.
You left too soon . . . too soon.
We never were intended to be
The Father's only boys, Krystar.
Your insane war and devastation
Were based on an arrogant presumption
That you were His chief son. Not so!
His only Son would be a Man
Who wears a robe of flesh.
I understood it all,
When man first stood in paradise.

"Is this world mine?" the creature shouted.

"Yours to care for . . . Yours to know,"
The Father-Spirit answered.
"Yes, beloved image of Myself.
Reign here, this world is kingdom, yes and crown!
Rise up, you plains, you mountains must kneel down.

You towering trees, strike every concourse dumb.
You ages glean, your fruit for years to come.
You oceans must pound out, "Myself . . . My Son!
A man is born, My Kingdom is begun."

The new man reached toward the open sky,
Dropped to his knees with hands upstretched.
He cried aloud the world's first words,
"Join every cleft, my new-born melody,
Oh, Terra, sing! And clap your hands, you trees.

"A thousand suns are wrapped in reverie
To see the force of love that I shall see."